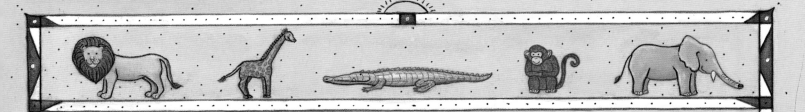

Hello Sun

A True African Travel Tale

written by Marcia Trimble • illustrated by Susan Arciero

Images Press - Los Altos Hills, California

Published by Images Press

No part of this publication may be reproduced, or stored in a retrieval system, or transmitted in any form or by any means, electronic, mechanical, photocopying, recording, or otherwise, without permission of the publisher.
For information regarding permission write to Images Press, 27920 Roble Alto Street, Los Altos Hills, California 94022

Publisher's Cataloging-in-Publication
(Provided by Quality Books, Inc.)

Trimble, Marcia.
    Hello sun / written by Marcia Trimble ;
illustrated by Susan Arciero. -- 1st ed.
    p. cm.
    Summary: A camera with a personality teaches children the fun of photography as it records images of lion cubs in Tanzania's Ngorongoro Crater for Malinda Martha to share with her friends at home.
    LCCN: 99-96580
    ISBN: 1-891577-50-6 (hc)
    ISBN: 1-891577-51-4 (pbk)

    1. Cameras--Juvenile fiction. 2. Lions--Juvenile fiction. 3. Photography--Juvenile fiction. 4. Ngorongoro Game Control Area Reserve (Tanzania)--Juvenile fiction.   I. Arciero, Susan. II. Title.

    PZ7.T7352He 2000   [E]
                  QBI99-1628

    10 9 8 7 6 5 4 3 2 1

Text was set in Comics Sans MS and Lemonade
Book design by MontiGraphics

Printed in Hong Kong by South China Printing Co. (1988) Ltd.
on totally chlorine-free Nymolla Matte Art paper.

For photography buffs and travelers alike
who especially enjoy seeing the world
through the eye of the camera.   - M.T.

For Benjamin.   - S.A.

Malinda Martha tucked Clicky
into her backpack
and bounced along in the landrover
bound for a game drive
in the Ngorongoro Crater.

"I have the greatest eye in the land," boasted Clicky
to himself. "Give me light. Lend me a hand."

At that moment...

Old Mama Simba was lying by the side of the road basking in the sun... asleep to the world.

She didn't see the landrover pull to a stop.

She didn't see Malinda Martha take Clicky out of the backpack and snap her picture.

Mama Simba didn't see Zabron Elias,
the safari guide from the HeHe tribe
of southern Tanzania,
point at something moving in the grasses
fifty yards away...

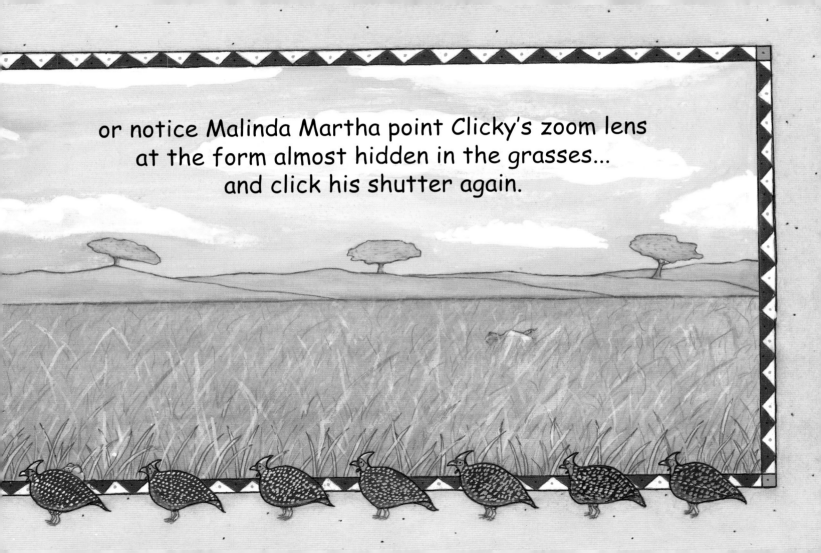

or notice Malinda Martha point Clicky's zoom lens
at the form almost hidden in the grasses...
and click his shutter again.

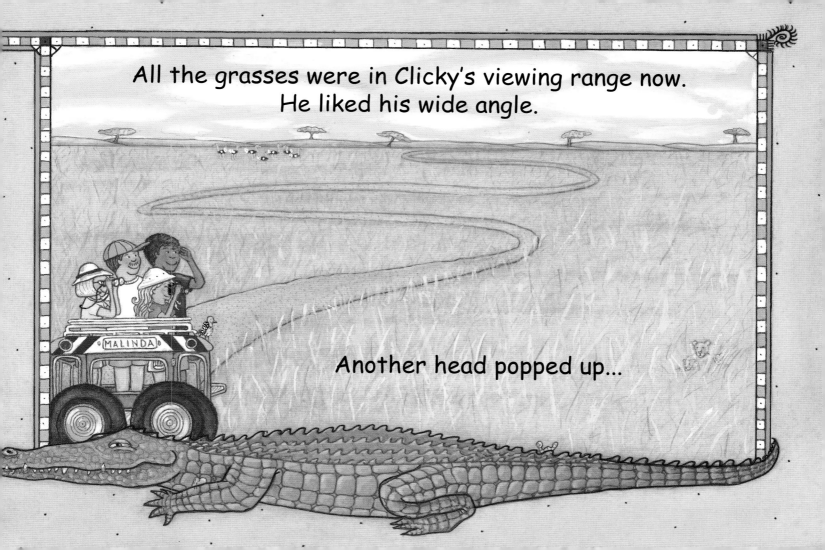

All the grasses were in Clicky's viewing range now.
He liked his wide angle.

Another head popped up...

AND another!

Clicky zoomed in on the cubs snuggling up to Mama Simba to nurse.

"Good morning sun...

"Good morning sun...
I have the greatest eye in the land," boasted Clicky to himself.

"Give me light. Lend me a hand.
I record memories for my fun.
I'm ready   for the cubs to run.

Good morning sun."

Other landrovers charged up. Tourists peered through their binoculars and clicked their shutters. Their point and shoot cameras didn't zoom like Clicky's.

Engines turned off and on, on and off...
and the tourists rode on.

Malinda Martha and Zeb did not drive on.
They watched. They waited.

Soon a lioness from the pride
came up the road

at   a   slow

steady   pace.

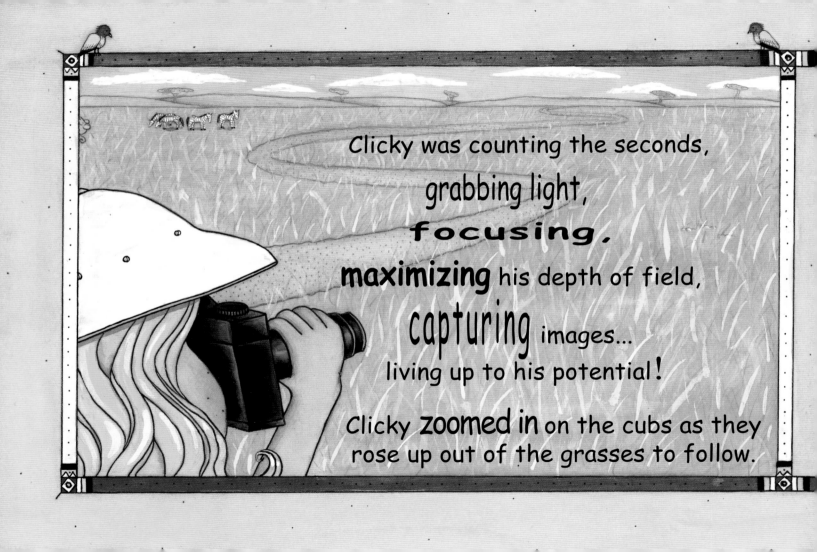

Clicky was counting the seconds,
grabbing light,
focusing,
maximizing his depth of field,
capturing images...
living up to his potential!

Clicky **zoomed in** on the cubs as they rose up out of the grasses to follow.

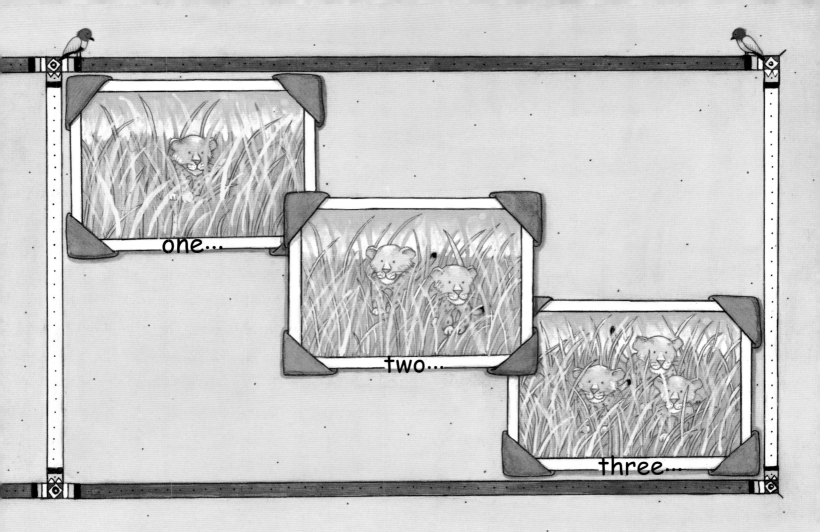

one...

two...

three...

four... "Four cubs!" Malinda Martha shouted, snapping Clicky's shutter again.

"Hello noonday sun...
I have the greatest
eye in the land,"
boasted Clicky to himself.
"Give me light.
Lend me a hand.
I record memories for my fun.
I'm ready for
the cubs to run.

Hello noonday sun."

Mama Simba and her cubs ran.
As they reached the brook at the side of
the road, the road filled with landrovers.
Mama Simba and her cubs ignored the
tourists and their clicking shutters.

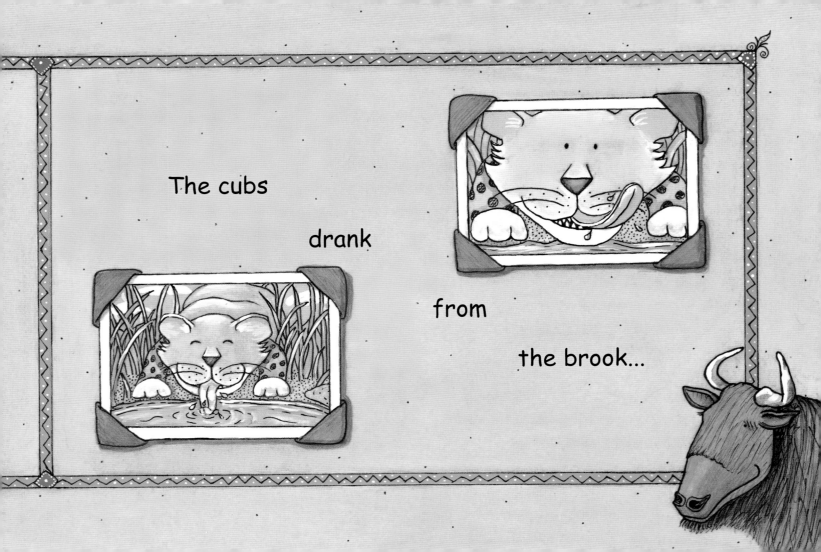

The cubs

drank

from

the brook...

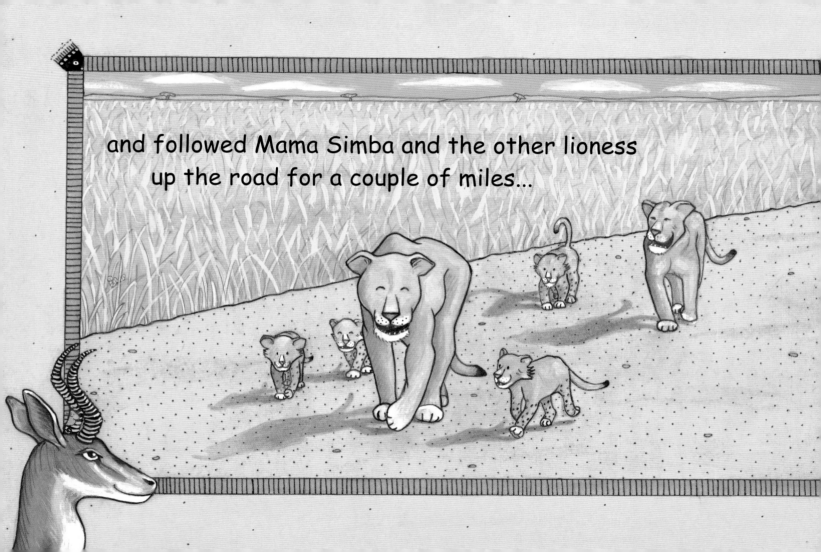

and followed Mama Simba and the other lioness
up the road for a couple of miles...

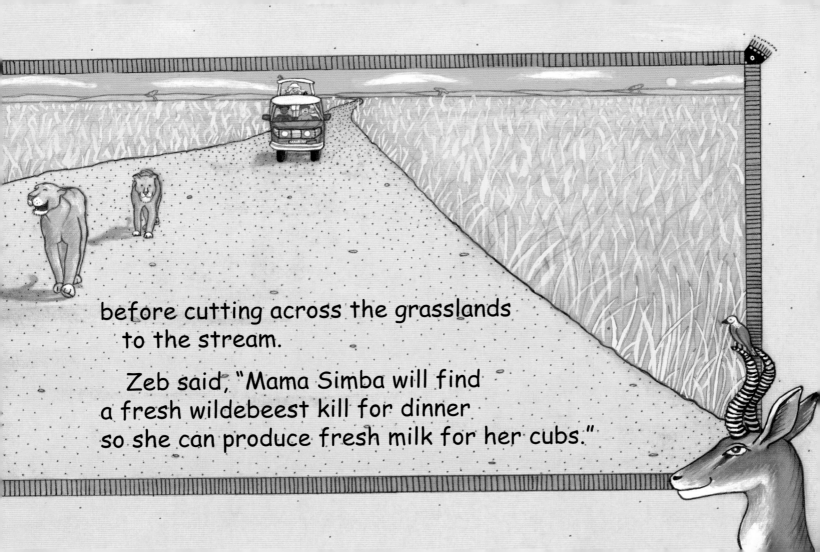

before cutting across the grasslands
   to the stream.

   Zeb said, "Mama Simba will find
a fresh wildebeest kill for dinner
so she can produce fresh milk for her cubs."

As the lion pride walked on across the grasslands,

out of Clicky's range,

Zeb turned the landrover around.

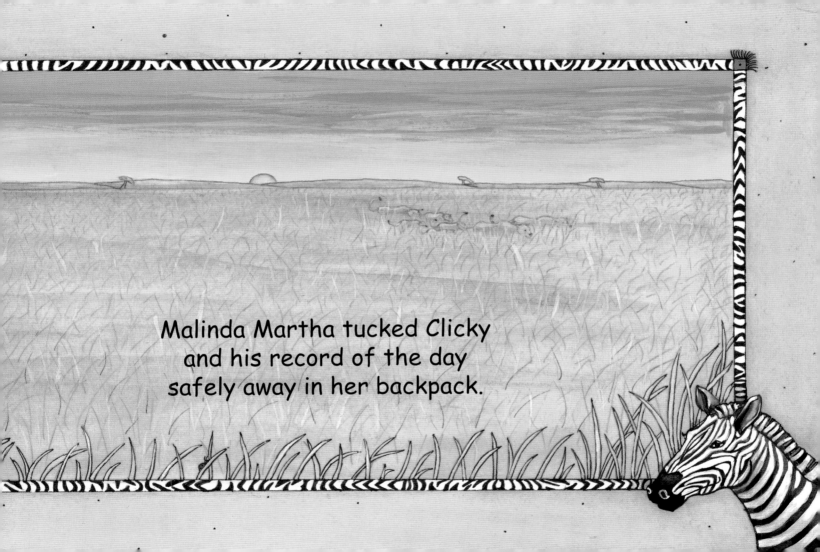

Malinda Martha tucked Clicky
and his record of the day
safely away in her backpack.

images for her to share
with her friends at home...

images

that

she would

always

hold

in her heart.

"Goodbye sun...
I have the greatest eye
in the land,"
Clicky boasted to himself.
"Give me light, lend me a hand.
I record memories for my fun
and rest my eye when day is done.
Goodbye sun."

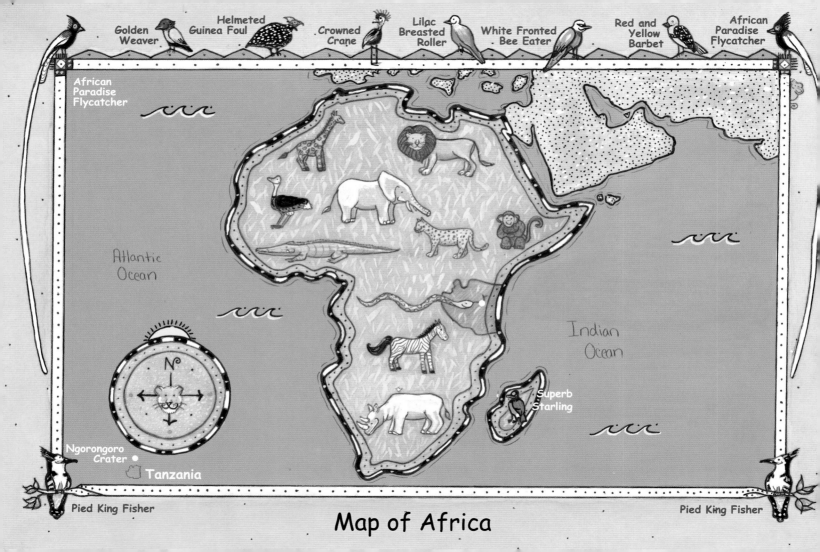

Map of Africa